The Meanest Mommy
is part of the DMB DeLIGHTful Development collection.

© Copyright 2024 by DM Butler. All rights reserved.
978-1-7324809-3-3
978-1-7324809-4-0

No part of this book may be reproduced or stored in a retrieval system, or transmitted in any form or by any means, electronic, mechanical, photocopying, or otherwise, without permission oof author.

Illustrated by Salma Ehab
© Copyright 2024

She makes me brush my hair

and every single morning
put on clean fresh underwear

Then when I'm dressed and ready
to finally have some fun
she makes me stop
and brush my teeth

My mommy says it's not okay
to eat fruit snacks all the time
but I'm not afraid of a tummyache
when there is lemon-lime

and strawberry and orange
yummy grape and tangerine
in chocolate sauce if I were boss
and my mommy weren't so mean

If my mommy used **MY** grocery list our cart would be filled with treats

maybe one bunch
of carrots or grapes ...
all that healthy stuff she eats

I would not make mommy blow on her soup just because it's hot

or zip her coat to stay warm outside
pinky swear that I would not

I sleep all night
so it's not alright
that she won't just let me play

I do not cross the street alone
she makes me hold her hand
I just can not get through to her
why won't she understand

My grandma says my mommy wants
what's best for me and so
I have to do the things she says
until I'm old enough, ya know

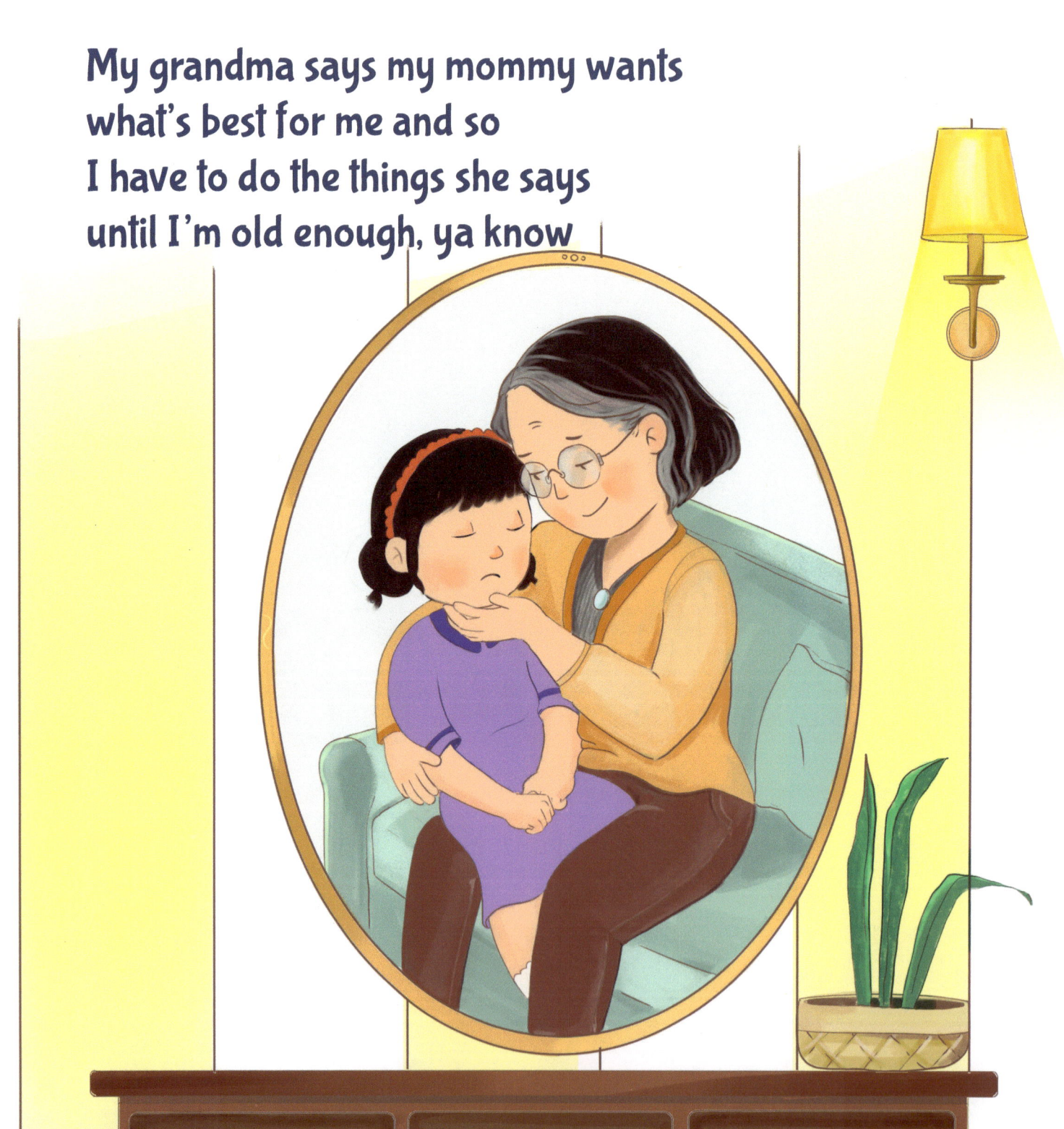

to have a kid and if I do

I won't make them do a thing

But then how will I keep them healthy ...

and warm ...

and safe ...

and clean?

and when they shout

I have The MEANEST MOMMY In the world !!!

I'll give them an extra hug
(like my mom does)

and an extra mommy smile

About the author:

DM Butler is an American author, and still the meanest mommy to three grown children who inspire stories that speak to the experiences, emotions, and questions shared by all of us at every stage of life, but from a particular point of view when walking through all of life's "firsts" with so much to consider: fear, loss, values, responsibilities, and love in all its beautiful forms.

Write to DM Butler at
dmbutlerwrites@gmail.com

More DeLIGHTful Development books by DM Butler:

I have this friend – A fun frolic through the fear of things that go bump in the night
The most magical thing of all – A story about the gifts our loved ones leave behind
The Wannabees – For everyone who ever wishes they could be like someone else
Be the change – A tribute to the words of Mahatma Ghandi on being our best selves
Daisy – An exploration of our personal and universal sense of belonging

Complete book list and DM Butler Inspirations (fauxtography and writings)
can be found at manitustudio.org

Buy here!

www.ingramcontent.com/pod-product-compliance
Lightning Source LLC
Chambersburg PA
CBHW040210100526
44585CB00002BA/109